Successories®

THE GREAT BIG
BOOK OF WISDOM

By
Brian Tracy

CAREER PRESS
Franklin Lakes, NJ

SUCCESSORIES®: THE GREAT BIG BOOK OF WISDOM
Cover design by Successories; Typesetting by Eileen Munson
Printed in the U.S.A. by Book-mart Press

To order this title, please call toll-free 1-800-CAREER-1 (NJ and Canada: 201-848-0310) to order using VISA or MasterCard, or for further information on books from Career Press.

The Career Press, Inc., 3 Tice Road, P O Box 687, Franklin Lakes, NJ, 07417

Library of Congress Cataloging-in-Publication Data

Tracy, Brian.
    The great big book of wisdom / by Brian Tracy.
        p.   cm.
    ISBN 1-56414-419-4 (hc.)
    1. Success.   I. Title.   II. Series.
BJ1611.2.T665   1999
158.1—dc21

99-21218

➤—*Self-Confidence*—➤

It is not lack of ability or opportunity that holds you back; it is only a lack of confidence in yourself.

There are no limits to what you can accomplish, except the limits you place on your own thinking.

Self-confidence is the foundation of all great success and achievement.

Average people have wishes and hopes. Confident people have goals and plans.

Confidence is a habit that can be developed by acting as if you already had the confidence you desire to have.

Imagine no limitations. What would you do with your life if you had all the education, experience, and resources that you require?

Idealize! Define the ideal future vision of your life in every detail.

What are you doing today that, knowing what you now know, you wouldn't get into again if you had to do it over?

You are always free to choose what you do more of, what you do less of, and what you do not at all.

Dream big dreams! Only big dreams have the power to move your mind and spirit.

"The key to success is to determine your goal and then act as if it were impossible to fail—and it shall be!"
—Dorothea Brande, American writer

How would you change your life if you won $1 million cash today? Whatever your answer, start today to take those actions.

Self-confident people do not compare themselves to others. They only compare themselves with the very best that they can be.

Commit yourself to excellence in every part of your life and never stop striving toward it.

"Boldness has genius, power and magic in it."
—Goethe

Fear and doubt are the major enemies of great success and achievement.

When you meet other people, look them in the eye, state your name clearly, and shake hands firmly.

The way you give your name to others is a measure of how much you like and respect yourself.

Expect to be successful, expect to be liked, expect to be popular everywhere you go.

You are nature's greatest miracle. There never has been and never will be anyone just like you.

Your name is the most important sound in your world. Give it with pride.

An attitude of positive self-expectancy is a great builder of confidence.

You do not need to be different from who you are. You only need to be *more* of the person you already are.

Define your life in your own terms and live every minute consistent with the very best person you can possibly be.

Your mind is like a muscle—the more you use it, the more powerful it becomes.

There is no problem you cannot solve, no obstacle you cannot overcome, and no goal you cannot achieve.

Anything anyone else has done, you can probably do as well, if you want to badly enough.

No one is better than you—some people are just better developed and more knowledgeable in certain areas.

In sales and business, the future belongs to the askers—the people who ask for what they want, over and over.

Ask for what you want. Ask for help, ask for input, ask for advice and ideas—but never be afraid to ask.

Ask politely. Ask expectantly. Ask positively. Ask warmly. Ask sincerely. Ask curiously. Remember, the future belongs to the *askers.*

Ask for the job you want. Ask for the salary you want. Ask for the responsibilities you want.

Take advantage of your employer. Take every opportunity to expand your skills and abilities.

Define your ideal lifestyle in every respect. What could you do today to begin creating it?

The first part of the word "triumph" is "try."

Confident people think, decide, and then take action. Be decisive!

Accept complete responsibility for every part of your life. Refuse to blame others or make excuses.

Accept that you are where you are and what you are because of yourself. If you don't like it, change it!

Face your problems squarely. As Shakespeare said, "Take arms against a sea of troubles, and in so doing, end them."

"If a thing is worth doing, it is worth doing badly."
—G. K. Chesterton

Anything worth doing is worth doing poorly at first, and often it's worth doing poorly several times until you master it.

Intelligence is a way of acting. If you act intelligently you are smart, regardless of your IQ.

You develop confidence by acting confidently and courageously when you could just as well play it safe.

Become an unshakable optimist—look for the good in every situation.

Fake it until you make it! Act as if you had all the confidence you require until it becomes your reality.

Seek for the valuable lesson in every setback or disappointment—you will always find one.

After every difficulty, ask yourself two questions: "What did I do right?" and "What would I do differently?"

The greatest human quality is that of becoming unstoppable! And you become unstoppable by refusing to quit, no matter what happens.

Talk to yourself positively all the time.
Keep repeating, "I can do it! I can do it!"
until your fears disappear.

"Do the thing you fear and the death of
fear is certain."
—Ralph Waldo Emerson

Self-doubt does more to sabotage individual potential than all external limitations put together.

Self-confidence is a learnable skill, like typing or riding a bicycle. You develop it with practice.

Whatever you think about grows in your life.

Building self-confidence is like building muscle—you start with the basic structure and then you build on it.

You are far more intelligent and creative than you realize. Resolve to get smarter and sharper every day.

Decide exactly what you want and resolve to persist, no matter what, until you achieve it.

You can achieve almost any goal if you just do what other successful people have done to achieve the same goals before you.

The key to success is for you to make a habit throughout your life of doing the things you fear.

"If you do not do the thing you fear, the fear controls your life."
—Glenn Ford, American actor

Everyone is afraid. The superior person is the one who acts in spite of his fears.

If you were totally unafraid of failure, what goals would you set for yourself?

If you did not care at all about what anyone else thought about you, what would you do differently, or change in your life?

Don't ever worry about what people might think. Other people aren't really thinking about you at all!

You are a thoroughly good person—
negative ideas you have about yourself
have no basis in reality.

Your thought is creative. Thoughts held in
mind, produce after their kind.

Clear written goals with plans of action
will build your self-confidence as fast as
any other factor.

"Believe in yourself; every heart vibrates to that iron string."
—Ralph Waldo Emerson

You are in an ongoing process of becoming, growing, and developing in the direction of your dominant thoughts. What are they?

Self-confident people think and talk about what they really want—and they tend to get it.

Whatever you believe with conviction becomes your reality. Choose your beliefs with care.

Challenge your self-limiting beliefs. Most of them are not true at all.

You experience calmness and confidence when you know you are doing the right thing—whatever it costs.

Confidence on the outside begins by living with integrity on the inside.

Be absolutely clear about who you are and what you stand for. Refuse to compromise.

Your self-confidence increases when you know you are living your life according to your highest values.

Companies with clear written statements of values and principles are more dynamic and profitable than those without. People, too.

What are your values? What do you stand for and believe in?

You can always tell your true values by looking at your behavior—especially under pressure.

You always evolve and develop in the direction of your dominant aspirations and your innermost convictions.

Self-confident people are very clear about who they are and what they believe in.

What is your vision for yourself and your life? Where do you want to be in five years?

>———◆———<

A clear vision, backed by definite plans, gives you a tremendous feeling of confidence and personal power.

People ignore what you say. They are only concerned with what you *do.*

The only measure of whether you truly believe something is how consistently you practice it.

Live your life in every way to earn and keep the respect of the people *you* respect.

Happiness and self-confidence come naturally when you feel yourself moving and progressing toward becoming the very best person you can possibly be.

Integrity is more than a value—it is the quality that guarantees all the other values.

Determine your unifying principles in life and resolve to live by them.

Unshakable self-confidence comes from unshakable commitment to your values.

If you were to write out your own obituary or eulogy, what would you want it to say about you after you die?

Organize your values by priority. What is more important to you? What is less important?

Set peace of mind as your highest goal and organize your entire life around it.

When you listen to your "inner voice" and follow your intuition, you will probably never make another mistake.

Resolve today to either resolve or walk away from any situation that makes you unhappy or causes you stress.

"People are just about as happy as they make up their minds to be."
—Abraham Lincoln

Denial is the root source of most mental illness. What is it in your life that you're not facing?

Self-confidence comes naturally when your inner life and your outer life are in harmony.

The more you do of what you're doing, the more you'll get of what you've got.

Deal with life the way it is, not the way you wish it could be.

High levels of self-confidence require that you always choose to live by a higher-order value rather than a lower-order value.

Accept yourself as a valuable and worthwhile person in every respect.

Speak about yourself in positive and constructive terms only. Never sell yourself short.

Intensity of purpose and commitment to a single goal or objective builds your self-confidence.

The most important values in life are contained in the people you love and the people who love you.

Every act of self-discipline increases your confidence, trust, and belief in yourself and your abilities.

"Self-confidence is the ability to make yourself do what you should do, when you should do it, whether you feel like it or not."
—Elbert Hubbard, author and lecturer

The great riches of life are self-esteem, self-respect, and personal pride—all based on self-confidence.

Persistence in the face of adversity builds your self-confidence and your ability to persist even more.

Persistence is self-discipline in action.

The natural tendency of all human behavior is toward the path of least resistance. When you resist this tendency, you become stronger and more powerful.

Persisting through lesser difficulties builds your capacity to persist through greater difficulties, and achieve even greater things.

*T*he more confident you are, the more you attract into your life people and circumstances that can help you to achieve your goals.

To build your confidence, repeat over and over, "I feel happy! I feel healthy! I feel terrific!"

Single-minded concentration toward your major goal gives you a sense of power, purpose, and self-direction.

The comfort zone is the great enemy of courage and confidence.

People with self-confidence set big goals for themselves in every area of life.

Setting big goals for yourself increases your confidence and your belief that they are attainable.

Your life is a reflection of your thoughts. If you change your thinking, you change your life.

"Our great fear is not that we are powerless, but that we are powerful beyond measure."
—Nelson Mandela, South African leader

Self-confidence is an attitude and
attitudes are more important than facts.

Visualize, imagine yourself as the calm,
confident, powerful person you really are
inside.

Think positively. The more optimistic you are, the more confident you become.

Every time you write out a goal, it increases your confidence that the goal is achievable for you.

Make every goal clear, specific, measurable, and time bounded.

The depth of your belief and the strength of your conviction determine the power of your personality.

The foundation of confidence in virtually every field is preparation.

Clarity is essential. Knowing exactly what you want builds your self-confidence immeasurably.

What have you always wanted to do but been afraid to attempt? Whatever it is, it may be your greatest opportunity in life.

Cast aside your doubts. Make a total commitment to living the life you were meant to live.

A feeling of confidence and personal power comes from facing challenges and overcoming them.

The more you learn and know in any area, the more confident you are.

Overlearning and overpreparing gives you the winning edge in any area.

Learn something new. Try something different. Convince yourself that you have no limits.

"There is no security in life, only opportunity."
—General Douglas MacArthur

You have within you, right now, the ability to be, have, and do far more than you've ever dreamed before.

You have been put on this earth to do something wonderful with your life.

The single common denominator of men and women who achieve great things is a sense of destiny.

Decide what's right before you decide what's possible.

"*C*ompared to what we could be, we are only half awake. We are making use of only a small part of our physical and mental resources. Stating the thing broadly, the human individual thus lives far within his limits. He possesses powers of various sorts which he habitually fails to use."

—William James, American philosopher

Imagine there were no limitations on what you could be, have, or do in any area of life. What goals would you set for yourself?

Committing your goals to paper increases the likelihood of your achieving them by 1,000 percent!

The foundation of lasting self-confidence
and self-esteem is excellence, mastery of
your work.

The better you are at what you do, the
more you like yourself and the greater is
your self-confidence.

Goals in writing are dreams with deadlines.

There are no unrealistic goals—only unrealistic deadlines.

Be a lifelong student. The more you learn, the more you earn and the more self-confidence you have.

You will only be truly happy and self-confident when you know you are really good at what you do.

What can you, and only you, do that if done well, will make a real difference in your life?

A motto for lasting self-confidence is, "Get good, get better, be the best!"

What is your "heart's desire?" What are you really meant to do with your life?

What activities, behaviors, or decisions have been most responsible for your success in life? Do more of them.

"*The power which resides in man is new in nature, and none but he knows what that is which he can do, nor does he know until he has tried.*"
—*Ralph Waldo Emerson*

The outer limit of your potential is determined solely by your own beliefs and your own confidence in what you think is possible.

Don't hold grudges. Refuse to blame anyone for anything that has happened in your life.

Accepting total responsibility for your life gives you a tremendous feeling of personal power and self-confidence.

Forgive everyone who has ever hurt you in any way. Let it go.

Do more than you are paid for. There are never any traffic jams on the extra mile.

Your success in life will be in direct proportion to what you do after you do what you are expected to do.

You are your most valuable asset. Take all the training you can get to increase your value.

Every great success is an accumulation of thousands of ordinary efforts that no one sees or appreciates.

Everything counts! Everything you do helps or hurts, adds up or takes away.

The harder you work, the luckier you get, and the more self-confidence you have.

When your goals are magnetized with the emotion of desire, you will experience what other people call "luck."

There are no shortcuts. To be a big success, start a little earlier, work a little harder, and stay a little later.

Resolve to pay any price or make any sacrifice to get into the top 10 percent in your field. The payoff is incredible!

You have the capacity to become very, very good in anything that is really important to you.

"Are you denying your greatness?"
—Les Brown, motivational speaker

A feeling of continuous growth is a wonderful source of motivation and self-confidence.

Invest 3 percent of your income back into yourself in the form of continuous learning.

There is nothing that can stop you from getting to the top of your field—except yourself.

Read an hour every day in your chosen field. This works out to about one book per week, 50 books per year, and will guarantee your success.

Listen to audio programs in your car. This works out to 500 to 1,000 hours per year of high-quality education—better than attending university.

Continuous learning is the minimum requirement for success in your field.

High levels of competence and mastery in your field will give you a feeling of unshakable self-confidence.

Get around the right people. Associate with positive, goal-oriented people who encourage and inspire you.

Self-confidence requires high levels of health and energy.

"Fatigue doth make cowards of us all."
—Vince Lombardi, football coach

Be selective about what you see, watch, hear, and listen to. Keep your external influences predominantly positive.

You can accomplish virtually anything if you want it badly enough and if you are willing to work long enough and hard enough.

Television can be a wonderful tool or a terrible master, depending on what you watch, and how you watch it.

See and think of yourself as a leader
and then do what leaders do. Dare to
go forward.

Be a *creator* of circumstances rather
than just a *creature* of circumstances.
Be proactive rather than reactive.

A sense of control is essential to a feeling of self-confidence and a positive mental attitude.

Take complete control over the messages you allow into your conscious mind.

Control your inner dialogue. Talk to yourself positively all the time.

Visualize and think about yourself as you would ideally *like* to be, not just as you are.

It is not what happens to you, but how you respond to what happens to you that determines how you feel.

Decide in advance to respond positively and constructively to every adversity.

Develop an attitude of positive self-expectancy, confidently expecting to gain something from every situation.

Avoid negative people at all costs. They are the greatest destroyers of self-confidence and self-esteem.

*H*appiness is the progressive realization
of a worthy goal or ideal. Do something
to move toward your goals every single
day.

If your happiness is dependent on someone changing, you are bound to be disappointed.

Confident people are willing to take risks; people who take risks develop self-confidence.

The better you get along with other people, the better you feel about yourself.

The best words for resolving a disagreement are, "I could be wrong; I often am." It's true.

"Don't ask for things to be easier; ask instead for you to be better."
—Jim Rohn, success philosopher

Most of your happiness will come from your relationships with others. Handle them with care.

Develop an "attitude of gratitude": Be thankful for every good thing in your life.

The more you like and respect yourself, the more you like and respect others, and the more they like and respect you.

Your self-confidence is directly connected to how much you feel you are making a difference in your world.

Whenever you do something nice for someone else, your self-esteem and self-confidence go up proportionately.

Single-minded concentration in the direction of your dreams intensifies your desires and increases your self-confidence.

Treat each person with consideration, caring, and courtesy—and watch your confidence soar!

Practice the body language of self-confidence. Stand tall and straight with your chin high and walk briskly. You will feel better and act better.

Every time you say "thank you" to another person, they feel better and so do you.

Everything that you do or say that raises the self-esteem of another raises yours as well.

Total commitment to a relationship builds your confidence and self-esteem.

Make others feel important. The more important you make them feel, the more important you feel, as well.

Complete acceptance of yourself as a valuable and worthwhile person is a real self-esteem builder.

Everyone earns their living by selling something to someone. How good are you?

Your ability to persuade and influence others determines the quality of your life, and your self-confidence.

Learning to speak in public will increase your self-confidence dramatically.

Your self-confidence will be determined by the people you surround yourself with as much as by any other factor.

The more effective you are with people, the calmer and more confident you will feel.

Life is too short to waste a minute of it doing a job you don't like or care about.

Confidence comes from being prepared to cut your losses, to walk away from a bad situation.

If you were not doing your current job today, would you apply for it? Would you get it?

"*Courage is rightly considered the foremost of the virtues, for upon it, all others depend.*"
—*Winston Churchill*

The ideal job for you is usually easy to learn and easy to do. You can hardly wait to get there.

If you don't want to be excellent at your current job, it's probably not the right job for you.

Choose a field you enjoy and then become totally absorbed in it.

Where do you want to be in five years? Is what you are doing right now going to get you there?

Determine your personal *Area of Excellence.* How can you best capitalize on it?

Be prepared to reinvent yourself every year. Imagine starting over with no limitations or encumbrances.

Learn to negotiate in your best interests. It makes you feel terrific.

Be a great listener. Ask questions and listen intently to the answers.

Self-confidence requires having the courage to live your life in your own way.

High levels of self-confidence come from the feeling that you are the master of your own destiny.

You have far more weaknesses than strengths—concentrate always on your strengths.

Concentrate on one thing, the most important thing, and stay with it until it's complete.

Think on paper. Set priorities and always work on your highest-value tasks.

In times of turbulence and rapid change, you must constantly be re-evaluating yourself relative to the new realities.

Self-confidence comes when you are working at peak levels of efficiency and effectiveness.

The more high-value tasks you accomplish, the more powerful and positive you feel.

Keep setting new and higher goals and standards for yourself. Never be satisfied.

Take control over your environment and ensure that it is predominantly positive.

A feeling of significance arises in you when you know that you are making a difference in the world.

Never settle for anything less than your best.

"Persistence is to the character of man as carbon is to steel."
—Napoleon Hill, success author

Your ability to function well in the inevitable crisis is the true measure of the person you are.

Life is a continuous succession of problems. The only question is how you respond to them.

You can develop any quality that you desire to achieve any goal that you set for yourself.

What is your *Limiting Step*? What is holding you back from the life you desire?

Work at least as hard on yourself as you do on your job.

You have more talent and ability than you could ever use in an entire lifetime.

*M*ake a game of finding something
positive in every situation—95 percent
of your emotions are determined by
how you interpret events to yourself.

Desire is the only real limit on your abilities.

"There are powers inside of you, which, if you could discover and use, would make of you everything you ever dreamed or imagined you'd become."
—Orison Swett Marden, success author

Act boldly, and unseen forces will come to your aid.

When you want something badly enough, you will develop the confidence and the ability to overcome any obstacle in your way.

Resolve in advance to persist until you succeed, no matter what the difficulty.

To keep yourself positive and self-confident, think about your goals all the time.

Flood your mind with positive words, images, books, tapes, and conversations.

If you can dream it, you can do it. Your limits are all within yourself.

When you absolutely believe in yourself and your ability to succeed, nothing will stop you.

Successful people make a habit of decisiveness in everything they do.

There is nothing wrong with making mistakes. Learning from mistakes is how we grow.

The Law of Cause and Effect is the iron law of human destiny. Thoughts are causes, and conditions are effects.

The history of the human race is the history of ordinary people who have overcome their fears and accomplished extraordinary things.

Your level of optimism is determined by how you explain things to yourself. Think positively.

Carpe diem. Seize the day! Do the thing and you will have the power.

"Courage is not absence of fear, lack of fear. It is control of fear, mastery of fear."
—Mark Twain

To discover new continents, you must be willing to lose sight of the shore.

Failure is an indispensable prerequisite for success. It is how you learn the lessons you need.

Remember, you only have to succeed the last time.

Live in truth with all people under all circumstances.

Continually set higher standards for yourself, knowing confidently that you can reach them.

Deal honestly and objectively with yourself; intellectual honesty and personal courage are the hallmarks of great character.

Success comes in *cans*, not in *can'ts.*

Treat yourself as a lifelong "do-it-to-yourself" project. Strive for feelings of inner harmony, balance, and peace of mind.

Whatever you can do, or dream you can, begin it.

"*If a man advances confidently in the direction of his dreams, he will experience a success unknown in common times.*"
—*Henry David Thoreau, American philosopher*

Personal Achievement

You have great, untapped reserves of potential within you. Your job is to release them.

It doesn't matter where you're coming from; all that matters is where you are going.

Imagine your life is perfect in every respect; what would it look like?

There are no limits on what you can achieve with your life, except the limits you accept in your own mind.

Everything you do in life is either to get love, or to compensate for lack of love.

Learn from the experts; you will not live long enough to figure it all out for yourself.

Life is like a combination lock; your goal is to find the right numbers, in the right order, so you can have anything you want.

If you do the right things in the right way, you will get whatever results you desire.

Your most valuable asset can be your willingness to persist longer than anyone else.

If you want to achieve greatly in life, be a student of achievement.

Nature is neutral; if you do the same things that other successful people have done, you will inevitably enjoy the same success they have.

Almost all your unhappiness in life comes from your tendency to blame someone else for something.

Decide exactly what you want in every area of your life; you can't hit a target you can't see.

Any system or blueprint for success is better than none at all. Think on paper.

Virtually anything you could ever want to be, have, or do is achievable with learning and hard work.

Make your life a masterpiece; imagine no limitations on what you can be, have, or do.

Make a decision today to do something wonderful with your life.

Your inner voice will ultimately guide you to say and do the right things at the right time.

You have the ability, right now, to exceed all your previous levels of accomplishment.

Delay gratification. Resist the urge to spend everything you earn, plus a little bit more every month.

Accumulate a minimum of three months' expenditures in a safe place—and never touch it.

The habit of regular saving plus the miracle of compound interest will make you rich.

Make your own financial decisions. Never depend on anyone else.

Engage in "mountaintop thinking"; project forward in thought and imagine your ideal life. What does it look like?

If you are worried about money, it simply means that you can and should be earning more. How are you going to do it?

Make your financial independence a primary goal in life and begin working toward it today.

Pay yourself first! Save 10 percent or more of your gross income every single paycheck.

Money is hard to earn and easy to lose. Guard yours with care.

The kindest thing you can do for the people you care about is to become a happy, joyous person.

You can't give away something that you don't have; you can't make others happy if you are unhappy.

You are successful to the degree to which you can attain your own happiness.

You are positive, creative, and happy to the degree to which you eliminate negative emotions from your life.

"Only one life, that soon is past; only what's done with love will last."
—Anonymous

Be willing to launch in faith, with no guarantees of success. This is the mark of personal greatness.

You are always free to choose what you do with your life. To make changes in your future, make new choices today.

Decide today to design and build the ideal relationship in your life. It's up to you.

Most of your happiness, and your unhappiness, comes with hair on top, and talks back.

Resist the temptation to defend yourself or make excuses.

The great secret of success is that there are no secrets of success; there are only timeless principles that have proven effective throughout the centuries.

The amount you laugh in your relationships with others is the true measure of the health of your personality.

Design your financial future in every respect, and then make a plan to achieve it.

Time is money; continually look for ways to do things faster and better.

We live in the richest society in all of human history; are you getting your fair share?

Decide how much you want to be earning one year, five years and ten years from today. What will you have to do to achieve these amounts?

You are only as free as your options;
develop alternatives to every situation.

To be truly happy, you need a clear sense
of meaning and purpose in life.

An attitude of calm, confident
expectation activates your creativity
and unlocks your mental powers.

Make a commitment today to something bigger and more important than yourself.

Self-actualization and self-fulfillment result when you feel that you are becoming everything that you are capable of becoming.

Happiness is the progressive realization of a worthy ideal.

To perform at your best, you need to know who you are and why you think and feel the way you do.

If necessity is the mother of invention, pain seems to be the father of learning.

You are not what you think you are; but what you think, you are! You always behave, on the outside, in a manner consistent with your self-concept, on the inside.

The success you are enjoying today is the result of the price you have paid in the past.

Life is hard; it always has been and it always will be. Accepting this reality somehow makes it easier.

Failure is an absolute prerequisite for success. You learn to succeed by failing.

Destructive criticism in childhood causes you to fear failure and rejection as an adult.

Action-orientation, the willingness to move fast when opportunity presents itself, is the key quality for success in every area.

All change in your life comes when your mind collides with a new idea.

Anything you can hold in your mind on a continuing basis, you can have.

You are a potential genius; there is no problem you cannot solve, and no answer you cannot find somewhere.

Your multi-dimensional brain is influenced by everything you see, hear, read, smell, touch, feel, or say. Be careful.

Take charge! You feel positive about yourself to the exact degree to which you feel you are in control of your own life.

For every effect in your life, there is a specific cause. There is a reason for everything.

Decide in advance to use every adversity or setback as a spur to greater effort.

Set high goals and standards for yourself; resist the temptation of the comfort zone.

*P*eace of mind is the highest human good and it is your normal, natural condition. Ask yourself, "Do you want to be right, or do you want to be happy?"

Live in harmony with your highest values and your innermost convictions. Never compromise.

If there is anything you want in life, find out how others have achieved it and then do the same things they did.

You learn to love others by doing loving things with and for them.

Thoughts are causes and conditions are effects. You are creating your current life with your present thinking.

The one thing over which you have complete control is your thinking; use it well.

If there is something in your life you do not want, find the cause and remove it.

Setting deadlines for your goals activates your subconscious mind and reinforces your determination.

Smile. Everyone you meet is carrying a heavy load.

Whatever you believe, with conviction, becomes your reality, whether or not it is true or false.

You must become the person you want to be on the inside before you see the appearance of this person on the outside.

Develop a benevolent world view; look for the good in the people and circumstances around you.

The biggest mental roadblocks that you will ever have to overcome are those represented by your self-limiting beliefs.

You can judge the validity of any idea or concept by asking, "Is this true for me?"

*Y*our brain has more than 100 billion cells, each connected to at least 20,000 other cells. The possible combinations are greater than the number of molecules in the known universe.

If you conduct yourself as though you expect to be successful and happy, you will seldom be disappointed.

If you were starting over today, what would you do differently? Whatever your answer, start doing it now.

Successful people are very clear about who they are and what they want.

Theodore Roosevelt said, "Do what you can, with what you have, right where you are." This is great advice.

Your true beliefs and values are only and always expressed in your actions, especially what you do under pressure.

You are in the people business, no matter what you do or where you do it.

Become an "inverse paranoid," someone who believes that the universe is conspiring to do you good.

Quickly say, "That's good!" to every setback and adversity, and then find out what is good about it.

Write out your goals on 3 x 5 index cards; review them twice each day.

Your incredible brain can take you from rags to riches, from loneliness to popularity, and from depression to happiness and joy—if you use it properly.

Everything you do is triggered by an emotion of either desire or fear.

Everything you have in your life you have attracted to yourself because of the person you are.

You can have more, be more, and do more because you can change the person you are.

You are where you are and what you are because of what you believe yourself to be. Change your beliefs and you change your reality.

"Two men looked out through prison bars; one saw the mud, the other saw the stars."

You have gone as far as you can today with your current level of knowledge and skill.

It is not failure itself that holds you back; it is the fear of failure that paralyzes you.

Thought is creative. You create your entire life with your thoughts, hour by hour and minute by minute.

It is when you finally learn that your fears are all in your mind that your real life begins.

Be positive; refuse to complain, condemn, or criticize anyone or anything.

The core of your personality is your self-esteem, "How much you like yourself." The more you like and respect yourself, the better you do at everything you attempt.

"Failure is merely another opportunity to more intelligently begin again."
—Henry Ford

Take control of your suggestive environment and only let in the words, images, and ideas you desire.

Your self-image controls your performance; see yourself as confident and in complete control.

You can only have as much love for yourself as you can express to others.

Good habits are hard to form but easy to live with; bad habits are easy to form but hard to live with.

Personality development is the process of building and maintaining high levels of self-esteem. You can change your performance by changing the way you think about yourself in that area.

Many of the most successful men and women in the world never graduated from college. They attended the "school of life" instead.

Your life today is the result of all of your choices and decisions in the past. When you make new choices, you create a new future.

Think continually in terms of the rewards of success rather than the penalties of failure.

Be future-oriented. When facing any problem, ask, "Where do we go from here?"

Self-esteem and self-love are the opposites of fear; the more you like yourself, the less you fear anything.

Make strong, affirmative statements to reinforce new, positive habit patterns of thought and behavior.

What one great thing would you dare to dream if you knew you could not fail?

You can develop any habit of thought or behavior that you consider desirable or necessary.

Continually bombard your mind with thoughts, words, pictures, and people consistent with the person you want to be and the goals you want to achieve.

You are inordinately influenced by those whose love and respect you most value.

Think continually about what you want, not about the things you fear.

Everything around you in the material world only has the meaning that you give to it with your thoughts.

Create your own poster, covered with pictures of the things you want to acquire. All improvement in your life begins with an improvement in your mental pictures.

You cannot control what happens; you can only control the way you respond to what happens.

"The greatest revolution of my life is the discovery that individuals can change the outer aspects of their lives by changing the inner attitudes of their minds."
—William James

Go on a 21-day PMA (Positive Mental Attitude) diet; think and talk about only the things you want for three weeks. This is not easy.

Excellence is not a destination; it is a continuous journey that never ends.

Affirming your desired goals is a way of telling the truth in advance.

Speaking aloud to yourself in a positive, confident way builds your self-confidence and improves your performance.

Take a deep breath, relax, and imagine yourself exactly as you wish to be.

Keep your conversation throughout the day consistent with what you really want to happen.

Visualize your goals and ideals continually, to influence your subconscious mind.

Act the part; walk and talk exactly as if you were already the person you want to be.

Feed your mind with mental protein, not mental candy. Read, listen to and watch positive, uplifting material.

Say the words, "I like myself!" over and over, 50 times a day.

Act with purpose, courage, confidence, competence, and intelligence until these qualities "lock in" to your subconscious mind.

Ignorance breeds fear; the more you learn about your subject, the less fear it holds for you.

The people you choose to associate with will determine your success as much as any other factor.

Associate with positive people, and get away from negative people.

The more you teach positive ideas to others, the better you learn them yourself.

Feeling listless? Make a list! Write down 10 things that you want to achieve in the next year.

Don't go out and just have a good day;
instead, make it a good day!

Stop talking about the problem and start
thinking about the solution.

Any idea or thought that you accept as
true will be accepted as a command by
your subconscious mind.

Your success will be largely determined by your ability to concentrate single-mindedly on one thing at a time.

Your conscious mind can only hold one thought at a time, positive or negative. Which is it going to be?

Your mind will make you rich or poor, depending on the uses you put it to.

Close your eyes, take seven deep breaths, and then visualize your most important goal as already a reality.

Play gentle, classical music when you read, study, or think about your goals.

Imagine that you are already the very best in your field; how would you behave differently? The fear of failure is the greatest single obstacle to success in adult life.

Emotionalize your mental images; your mental movies are your previews of life's coming attractions.

You can never rise higher than your expectations of yourself. Expect the best!

Wisdom is an equal combination of experience plus reflection. Take time to think about your life.

There are no extra human beings; you are here on this earth to do something special with your life.

Your ability to set goals and to make plans for their accomplishment is the master skill of success.

It is not what you say, or wish, or hope, or intend, it is only what you do that counts.

You can accomplish virtually any goal you set for yourself, as long as the goal is clear and you persist long enough.

Goals are the fuel in the furnace of achievement.

You are only happy when you are working toward a clear, specific goal of your own choosing.

True happiness and fulfillment come when you feel that you are making a valuable contribution to your world. What is yours?

"No one can make you feel inferior
without your consent."
—Eleanor Roosevelt

The only limitation on your ability is your
level of desire; how badly do you want it?

Each of us must develop an area of
excellence where he performs better
than almost anyone else.

Your subconscious mind cannot tell the difference between a real experience and one that you vividly imagine. Fool it.

"Intensity of purpose" is the distinguishing characteristic of high performing men and women.

The tendency to follow the path of least resistance guarantees failure in life.

You must decide exactly what is it you want in life; no one can do this for you.

Resolve that you will respond with a positive, optimistic, and cheerful mental attitude in every situation.

As you change the way you think on the inside, people and circumstances will change for you on the outside.

An attitude of positive expectation is the mark of the superior personality.

Clear goals allow you to control the direction of change in your life.

Combine your mental images with the emotion of desire to accelerate their realization.

You are already achieving every goal you are setting for yourself. Are you happy with your results?

Determine the price you are going to have to pay to achieve your goal, and then resolve to pay that price.

Look for something beneficial in every event that you can turn to your advantage.

Selecting your major definite purpose in life is the starting point of personal greatness.

Think about your goals at every opportunity throughout the day.

Start with a picture of your goal as already achieved in the future, and work back to the present. Imagine the steps that you would have taken to get from where you are now to where you want to be.

Ideas are a dime a dozen, but people to put them into effect are extremely rare.

If you swing hard enough and often enough you must eventually hit a home run.

Success equals goals; all else is commentary.

Keep your goals confidential; only tell people who are sympathetic to you, and who have goals of their own.

Success is a numbers game; there is a direct relationship between the number of things you try and your probability of ultimately succeeding.

Success comes when you do what you love to do and commit to being the best in your field.

Your greatest opportunity for success probably lies right under your own feet, your own acres of diamonds.

Opportunities usually come dressed in work clothes.

If you won $1 million, what work would you choose to do for the foreseeable future?

To enjoy perfect health, define what your life would be like if you already had it. Then do what you need to do to acquire it.

Imagine no limitations; decide what's right and desirable before you decide what's possible.

Organize your life around your values; what do you believe in and stand for?

Write down every goal you could want to accomplish in the next 10 years, then choose the most important one.

Intense, burning desire is the motivational force that enables you to overcome any obstacle and achieve almost any goal.

The people you love, and who love you, are the real measure of how well you are doing as a human being.

"What doesn't kill me makes me stronger."
—Friedrich Nietzsche

The north wind made the Vikings.

If you were absolutely guaranteed of success in any one thing, what one goal would you set for yourself?

What have you always wanted to do but been afraid to attempt? What fears are holding you back?

If every possible obstacle must first be overcome, nothing will ever get done.

The thrill of achievement comes from overcoming adversity in the accomplishment of an important goal.

Before you can achieve big goals, major efforts are necessary.

Nurture your faith and belief until they deepen into an absolute conviction that your goal is attainable.

Make a list of all the ways that you will personally benefit from achieving your goal.

The price of success must be paid in full, in advance.

Completely unrealistic goals are a form of self-delusion, and you cannot delude yourself into success.

Think before you begin. Prior planning prevents poor performance.

The simple act of writing down a goal and making a written plan for its accomplishment moves you to the top 3 percent.

Make your goals both realistic and achievable.

Those who do not have goals are doomed forever to work for those who do.

The more reasons you have for achieving your goal, the more determined you will become.

What is the biggest single obstacle that stands between you and your goal, right now?

"Stick to the fight when you're hardest hit; it's when things seem worst that you must not quit!"
—Anonymous

Goal setting is a science learned only by study, practice and application.

What additional knowledge and skill will you need to achieve your goal? Where can you acquire them?

Make a plan, a list organized by priority, to achieve your goal.

Make firm decisions about the things you want; burn your mental bridges behind you.

Rewrite your major goals every day, in the present tense, exactly as if they already existed.

The disease of "excusitis" is invariably fatal to success.

Your superconscious mind automatically and continuously solves every problem on the way to your goal.

Superior people take both the credit and the blame for everything that happens to them.

"*Whenever you find something getting done, anywhere, you will find a mono-maniac with a mission.*"
—*Peter Drucker*

Resolve to accept the worst, should it occur. Now you can stop worrying.

Whenever you set a goal of any kind, you will have to grow and develop to the point where you are ready to achieve it.

If you achieve your success without being prepared for it, you'll only end up looking foolish.

Most people achieved their greatest successes one step beyond what looked like their greatest failure.

When your goals are clear, you will come up with exactly the right answer at exactly the right time.

Self-responsibility is the core quality of the fully mature, fully functioning, self-actualizing individual.

Issue a blanket pardon. Forgive everyone who has ever hurt you in any way.

Forgiveness is a perfectly selfish act. It sets you free from the past.

View yourself as self-employed, the president of your own personal services corporation.

Whenever you feel angry or upset for any reason, neutralize the negative emotions by saying, "I am responsible!"

Eliminate worry by identifying the worst possible outcome of every situation.

Eliminating the expression of negative emotions is the starting point of rapid personal growth.

"I never hold grudges. While you're holding grudges, they're out dancing!"
—Buddy Hackett

When you are younger, you worry about what people think about you. When you are older, you realize that no one was ever thinking about you at all.

Repentance is good for the soul; apologize for anything you have done to hurt someone else.

Love only grows by sharing. You can only have more for yourself by giving it away to others.

If you're unhappy, what is it in your life that you're not facing?

Overconcern for the approval of others can paralyze your ability to take effective action.

Denial of some unpleasant reality lies at the core of most stress, unhappiness, and psychosomatic illness.

Most unhappiness is caused by a lack of clear meaning and purpose in your life.

There is always a price you can pay to be free of any unhappiness, and you always know what it is.

Once you start an important job, stay with it until it's 100-percent complete.

Winding up "unfinished business" with another person can give you a great burst of positive energy.

Which goal, if you accomplish it, will do more to help you achieve all your other goals?

What would you do, how would you spend your time, if you learned today that you only had six months to live?

Healthy, happy people are those who confront the facts of their lives directly.

Your personality is healthy to the degree to which you can get along with a variety of other people.

Any thought, plan, goal, or idea held continuously in your conscious mind must be brought into reality by your superconscious mind.

Stress and unhappiness come not from situations, but from how you respond to situations.

Nobody makes you angry; you decide to use anger as a response.

The fastest way to improve your relationships is to make others feel important in every way possible.

Identify and develop your unique talents and abilities, the things that make you special.

Be agreeable. It raises the self-esteem of others and makes you feel good about yourself.

Practice "white magic"; listen attentively to others when they speak.

Love of others begins with self-love and self-acceptance.

Develop an "attitude of gratitude." Say "thank you" to everyone for everything they do for you.

The way you get along with yourself will determine how well you get along with others.

Fully 95 percent of everything you think and feel is habitual and automatic, determined by past behaviors and experiences.

The only thing that you can never have too much of is love.

With relationships, either get in or get out. Make a total commitment, or go your own way.

The purpose of life is to develop loving relationships and to become a totally loving person.

You will be happy with another person to the degree to which you both share the same values, attitudes, ambitions, and beliefs.

Listening builds trust, the foundation of all lasting relationships.

Treat the people in your life as though they were the most important people in the world, because they are.

Always give without remembering and always receive without forgetting.

You are surrounded by a universal mind that contains all the intelligence, ideas and knowledge that have ever existed.

"We lie in the lap of an immense intelligence that responds to our every need."
—Ralph Waldo Emerson

Any good that you can do, do it now. Do not delay it or forestall it, for you will not pass this way again.

Why haven't you achieved your goals yet? What are your favorite excuses, and how do they hold you back?

The more you tell people that you love them, the more you love yourself.

Make a total commitment today, to yourself, your goals, and your relationships. Hold nothing back.

Become unstoppable by never stopping once you have started toward a goal that is important to you.

You only learn from feedback; the faster and more often you fail, the more rapidly you learn and succeed.

Your cybernetic brain mechanism will guide you unerringly to your goal, as long as the goal is clear.

Think of yourself as you wish to be, not as you are today.

The antidotes to fear and ignorance are desire and knowledge. Propel yourself forward by learning what you need to learn to do what you want to do.

Your success in life will be in direct proportion to what you do after you've done what is expected of you.

Within every setback or obstacle there is the seed of an equal or greater advantage or benefit. Find it.

Accept complete responsibility both for understanding and for being understood.

Make a decision! If that doesn't work, make another, and another, and another. Keep doing this until you break through.

The common characteristic of self-made millionaires is that they continually work harder and smarter than the average person.

Get out of your own way; most of your excuses for underachievement are figments of your imagination.

Goals that are not in writing are merely wishes or fantasies.

Knowledge is power, but only knowledge that can be applied to practical purposes in some way.

A horse that wins by a nose receives 10 times the prize money of a horse that loses by a nose. Little things mean a lot.

Practice "creative abandonment" of time-consuming activities that are no longer of importance to you.

Always work on the 20 percent of your activities that contribute 80 percent of your results. What are they?

The best songs are yet to be sung, the best stories are yet to be told, and the best years of your life lie ahead.

It is your attitude more than your aptitude that determines your altitude.

*B*ecome an unshakable optimist by thinking continually of the things you want, and by refusing to think about the things you fear.

You are surrounded right now by unlimited opportunities disguised as insurmountable problems.

Time is your most precious resource; make every minute count.

The golden rule is still the best principle for success: "Do unto others as you would have them do unto you."

"Lucky" people are simply those who think continually about what they want and then attract it into their lives.

The more positive you are when you think and work toward your goals, the faster you achieve them.

Never assume you understand. Ask the questions.

Be prepared to ride the cycles and trends of life; success is never permanent and failure is never final.

"You never can tell how close you are. You may be near when it seems so far."
—Anonymous

The future belongs to the competent; resolve to join the top 10 percent of people in your field and your future will be unlimited.

There are no accidents; success is the result of doing the right thing, in the right way, over and over.

Effective Leadership

Leaders are those who determine the
Area of Excellence for the group.

Leadership is the ability to get
extraordinary achievement from ordinary
people.

All work is done by teams; the leader's output is the output of his or her team.

Develop a bias for action, a Sense of Urgency, to get things done.

Ask yourself continually, "What can I and only I do that, if done well, will make a real difference?"

Fast tempo is essential for success; do it, fix it, try it!

◁ ✦ ▷

Identify your areas of strength and concentrate on those areas in which you can make a major contribution.

Lead the field! Start earlier, work harder, and stay later.

Simplify the task. Continually look for faster, better, easier ways to get the job done.

Practice Creative Procrastination with low-value tasks. Put them off indefinitely.

What is your Limiting Step? What sets the speed at which you accomplish your main goals?

"Inventory can be managed; people must be led—by example."
—Ross Perot

Do the unexpected. You are safer moving forward than standing still.

Clarity is the key to effective leadership. What are your goals?

Concentrate your powers. Identify what you are particularly good at doing and do more of it.

⊰ ✾ ⊱

Flexibility in a time of great change is a vital quality of leadership.

What are you trying to do? How are you trying to do it?

Be action-oriented! Lead, follow, or get out of the way.

Your ability to make good decisions will determine your success as much as any other factor.

Get the facts! Not the apparent facts, the assumed facts, or the hoped-for facts, but the real facts.

Errant assumptions lie at the root of every failure. What are yours? What if they are wrong?

"Men must be taught at the school of example, for they will learn at no other."
—Albert Schweitzer, humanitarian, Nobel prize winner

To achieve something you've never achieved before, you must become someone you've never been before.

Practice Tip-of-the-Iceberg-Thinking. Treat every unexpected event as if it were an indication of a trend.

Is there anyone working for you who, knowing what you now know, you wouldn't hire again?

Follow up and follow through until the task is completed, the prize won.

Face the world as it is, not as you wish it were.

Focus on your strengths. What are you uniquely capable of contributing to your situation?

‹ ❈ ›

Trust your intuition—listen to your inner voice.

Dare to go forward. Courage is the mark of greatness in leadership.

Refuse to make excuses or blame others. The leader always says, "If it's to be, it's up to me."

Identify your key result areas and then dedicate yourself to becoming very good in each one of them.

Imagine starting over. Think of reinventing yourself and your business every year.

Restructure your activities continually. Regularly move resources to higher-value activities.

Everyone is in the business of customer satisfaction. Who are your customers and how are you doing?

Continually tell people how good they are and what a great job they are doing.

Be willing to abandon your old ideas if someone comes up with something new and better.

"*If the rate of change outside your organization is greater than the rate of change inside your organization, then the end is in sight.*"
—Jack Welch, CEO General Electric Company

Leaders set high standards. Refuse to tolerate mediocrity or poor performance.

Apply the 80/20 Rule to everything you do. What are your highest-value activities?

Superior executives amaze and delight their customers. Do you?

The average person works at 50 percent or less of potential. Your job is to unleash that extra 50 percent.

The most powerful and predictable people-builders are praise and encouragement.

Quality is what the customer says it is. How do your customers define quality?

Good leaders make sure that everyone knows what is expected, every single day.

Do you care about me? Answer this question of your staff on every possible occasion.

Manage by objectives. Tell people exactly what you want them to do and then get out of their way.

Manage by exception. Only require reporting when there is a deviation from the plan.

Manage by responsibility. It is a powerful way to grow people.

The best leaders have a high Consideration Factor. They really care about their people.

Practice the philosophy of continuous improvement. Get a little bit better every single day.

Develop the winning edge; small differences in your performance can lead to large differences in your results.

Take time to listen to your people when they want to talk. This is a real motivator.

Develop a clear vision for your organization. Where do you want to be in five years?

What are your values? What do you stand for? Does everyone know?

What is your mission? Why does your organization exist at all?

Dedicate yourself to continuous personal improvement—you are your most precious resource.

The quality of your ideas will be in direct proportion to the quantity of ideas you generate.

Failing to plan means planning to fail. What are your goals?

The best leaders are the most attentive to detail. Leave nothing to chance.

Management is a mental game. The better you think, the greater the results you'll achieve.

Ask yourself regularly, "What is the most valuable use of my time right now?"

Delegate the right job to the right person at the right time, and be ready to change quickly.

Deploy yourself for maximum Return on Energy. Focus on your strengths.

Choose your people with care. Proper selection is 95 percent of success as a leader.

"You can never solve a problem with the same kind of thinking that created the problem in the first place."
—Albert Einstein

Always focus on accomplishments rather than activities.

Outstanding leaders have a sense of mission, a belief in themselves and the value of their work.

The best time to let a person go is usually the first time you think about it.

Empower others to perform at their best by continually reminding them how good they are and how much you believe in them.

⊰ ❁ ⊱

Why are you on the payroll? What have you specifically been hired to do?

Keep people informed. Everyone wants to know what's really going on.

What one skill, if you developed it to a high level, would have the greatest positive impact on your career?

The functions of the executive are innovation and marketing. How much time do you spend on each?

The leader accepts high levels of personal responsibility for performance and results.

‹ ❈ ›

Leaders think and talk about the solutions. Followers think and talk about the problems

The leader acts as though everyone is watching even when no one is watching.

The effective leader recognizes that she is more dependent on her people than they are on her. Walk softly.

Reinforce what you want to see repeated: What gets rewarded gets done.

Superior leaders are willing to admit a mistake and cut their losses. Be willing to admit that you've changed your mind. Don't persist when the original decision turns out to be a poor one.

Continually focus your energies on the one or two things that represent real pay-off opportunities.

Always choose the future over the past. What do we do now?

Think on paper. All highly effective executives think with pen in hand.

When picking people for your team, the best rule is, "Hire slowly and fire fast."

⟨❀⟩

Fast people decisions are almost invariably wrong people decisions. Take your time.

Once you have a clear objective, think
and talk only in terms of "How?"

Self-selection is an excellent measure.
Only hire people who really want the job.

Be perfectly selfish when you hire
somebody. Only select people you like,
enjoy, and want to be around.

Obstacles are what you see when you take your eyes off your goals.

Write out a clear, detailed description of the ideal candidate before you begin interviewing new people.

Attitude and personality are as important as experience and ability. Choose wisely.

The only real predictor of future performance is past performance. Check references carefully.

Praise is a powerful people-builder. Catch individuals doing something right.

"*I keep six honest serving men
(They taught me all I knew);
Their names are What and
Why and When
And How and Where and Who.*"
—*Rudyard Kipling*

People need regular feedback to know how they are doing and to keep on track.

The number-one demotivator in the world of work is not knowing what is expected.

The two major sources of value today are time and knowledge. Find new ways every day to use them better.

The key responsibility of leadership is to think about the future. No one else can do it for you.

Set clear goals and standards for each person. What gets measured gets done.

Set deadlines and sub-deadlines for all assignments.

Delegation is not abdication—inspect what you expect.

Start new hires off strong. Load them with responsibilities from the first day.

Keep everyone involved. Hold regular meetings to discuss the work.

⋖ ❀ ⋗

"If you don't have competitive advantage, don't compete!"
—Jack Welch, CEO General Electric Company

Leadership is the ability to get followers. Do people follow you willingly?

Practice Golden-Rule Management in everything you do. Manage others the way you would like to be managed.

People can do amazing things if they are well-managed and properly motivated.

Respect is the key determinant of high-performance leadership. How much people respect you determines how well they perform.

Be a life-long learner. Engage in daily self-renewal.

Take excellent care of your physical health. Energy and vitality are essential to effective leadership.

"The first hour is the rudder of the day." —Henry Ward Beecher

Reading one hour every day in your field will give you the edge over your competition.

Crisis is inevitable. The only thing that matters is how you deal with it when it comes.

Intellectual capital is the most valuable of all factors of production.

Practice *Crisis Anticipation* regularly. Think about what could possibly go wrong and then provide against it.

Continuous learning is the minimum requirement for success in your field.

Think! There is no problem that is not amenable to the power of sustained thinking.

The three "C's" of leadership are Consideration, Caring, and Courtesy. Be polite to everyone.

"Circumstances do not make the man;
they merely reveal him to himself."
—Epictetus, Roman philosopher

The value of a promise is the cost to you
of keeping your word.

Leaders think and talk in terms of
excellence. This means "Be the Best!"

What is your next job going to be? What additional knowledge and skills will you need to perform excellently in that position?

Those who do not think about the future cannot have one.

Your weakest important skill sets the height at which you use all your other skills.

Become computer literate. Use technology to leverage your abilities.

"The very best way to predict the future
is to create it."
—Michael Kami, strategic planner

Whatever got you to where you are today
is not enough to keep you there.

What one factor slows the speed at which you achieve your goals? How can you alleviate this constraint?

Keep raising the bar on yourself. How can you better serve your customers today?

To earn more, you must learn more.

The chief distinguishing characteristic of leaders is *Intensity of Purpose.*

≺ ❀ ≻

Leaders concentrate single-mindedly on one thing—the most important thing, and they stay at it until it's complete.

Simplify, consolidate, and eliminate tasks. Reengineer your work continuously.

Leaders tap into the emotions of their people by getting excited themselves.

Leadership is more who you are than what you do.

"*To thine own self be true and then, it must follow, as the night the day, thou canst not then be false to any man.*"
—*Shakespeare*

Integrity is the most valuable and respected quality of leadership. Always keep your word.

Character is the ability to follow through on a resolution long after the emotion with which it was made has passed.

Action orientation is the mark of the superior executive.

Keep asking yourself, "What kind of a company would my company be if everyone in it was just like me?"

There are no bad soldiers under a good general.

Managers have the ability to get results; leaders have a vision of the future.

The job of a leader is to assure excellent performance of the business task.

What could you do to speed up the process of delivering products and services to your customers?

Outsource every function and activity that can possibly be done better by someone else.

Different people require different leadership styles at different times in their careers.

Give inexperienced staff firm direction and clear guidance.

"Feedback is the breakfast of champions."
—Ken Blanchard, management writer

Coach and counsel continually to build top performers.

Encourage participation and involvement from everyone in the accomplishment of complex tasks.

Delegate responsibility only to those who have demonstrated the capacity to handle it.

Take time to think and reflect. Thoughtfulness is a key quality of successful leaders.

Dare to go forward! Have you ever tried pushing a string?

You are where you are and what you are because of yourself, because of your own choices and decisions.

Benchmark your performance against your best competitors. Think how you can beat them next time.

Leaders are never satisfied; they continually strive to be better.

Success can lead to complacency, and complacency is the greatest enemy of success.

In a time of rapid change, standing still is the most dangerous course of action.

"Any addition to the truth subtracts
from it."
—Aleksandr Solzhenitsyn,
   Russian Nobel prize winning author

A weakness is often a strength
inappropriately applied. Move people
around from one job to the other.

Create a new position if you have a talented person with a specific skill.

Avoid the comfort zone of the low performer. Set your standards higher and higher.

Practice management by walking around to get timely information and feedback.

Your success depends upon the whole-hearted commitment to excellence on the part of everyone who reports to you.

A single person who lacks commitment can be a major source of problems in your organization.

Be prepared to modify the task or change the individual if necessary.

Practice Blue-Sky Thinking: Imagine you could do anything. What would you do differently?

Resist reverse or upward delegation.
Don't let others hand the job back to you.

◄ ❀ ►

Leaders are demanding task masters.
They insist that the job be done right.

Decide upon your major definite purpose
in life and then organize all your
activities around it.

Leaders accept complete responsibility
for themselves in every part of their lives.

"Never complain, never explain."
—Benjamin Disraeli, British Prime
   Minister

Practice being a mentor to your staff.
Give them guidance to advance their
careers.

◁ ❀ ▷

Set an example in everything you do—
everyone is watching.

Invest in ongoing training and development of your staff.

Loyalty is one of the most valuable traits of the effective executive—to your company, your boss, and your staff.

Set clear priorities on everything before you begin.

*The purpose of an organization
is to maximize individual strengths
and make weaknesses irrelevant.*

High performance people are dependent on high-quality relationships with their bosses.

Truthfulness is the real mark of integrity.

Dress for success. Image is very important. People judge you by the way you look on the outside.

Remember the Law of the Excluded Alternative: Doing one thing means not doing something else.

Setting priorities means setting posteriorities as well. What should you be doing less of?

Long-term potential consequences are the true measure of priorities on every activity.

Create an atmosphere of openness, honesty, and straight talk around you.

Make one person responsible for each key result area.

Write down clear, specific goals for each area of your life.

◄ ❀ ►

"If you don't know where you're going, any road will get you there."
—Thomas Carlyle, British philosopher

Identify your critical success factors—the things you absolutely, positively have to do well to be successful.

Do what you love to do and commit yourself to doing it in an excellent fashion.

Your customer is anyone who depends on you, or who you depend upon for success.

Your ability to solve problems effectively determines how high you rise in your career.

Your company's most valuable asset is how it is known to its customers.

If your job is customer satisfaction, your real job title is *Problem-Solver.*

How do your customers think about you and talk about you when you're not there?

Perception is reality. Everything you do affects perceptions in some way.

< ❀ >

Only undertake what you can do in an excellent fashion. There are no prizes for average performance.

Leaders do not always make the right decisions, but they make their decisions right.

Leaders take the time to teach junior employees how to do the job well.

Management enables you to move from what you can do to what you can control.

Unlock your inborn creativity; always be searching for newer, better, faster ways to get the job done.

See yourself as self-employed. Treat the company as if you owned the place.

Identify your unique talents and abilities.
What has been most responsible for your
success in life, to date?

Effective leaders begin not with
themselves, but with the needs of the
situation. What are they?

Top performing leaders accept feedback
and self-correct.

Imagine no limitations on what you could do. Practice "back from the future" thinking. Project forward five years and look back.

Think on paper. Every minute spent in planning saves 10 minutes in execution.

Develop the mindset of peak performance. Repeat, "Back to work!" over and over again.

Always be willing to consider the possibility that you could be wrong.

The true test of leadership is how well you function in a crisis.

⊰❀⊱

Your ability to solve problems and make good decisions is the true measure of your skill as a leader.

Leaders stay calm, cool, and collected in the face of danger and difficulty.

Never come across as impatient; always be relaxed, cheerful, and positive—even if you're all wound up inside.

Intense result orientation is the mark of the superior executive.

Listen to stress and use it as a friend to tell you what parts of your life are out of alignment with your true nature.

Power and influence derive from the ability to help or hurt others.

The future belongs to the risk-takers, not the comfort-seekers.

Spend 80 percent of your time focusing on the opportunities of tomorrow rather than the problems of yesterday.

Everyone is afraid. The leader is the person who masters the fear and acts in spite of the fear.

Analyze each situation by asking, "What is the worst possible thing that could happen?" Then make sure that it doesn't happen.

To motivate others to peak performance, continually make them feel important and valuable.

Leaders create a work environment in which people feel terrific about themselves.

Practice brainstorming with your staff on a regular basis. Keep them thinking creatively about the job.

Time is perishable; it cannot be saved. It can only be spent in different ways.

Time is irreplaceable; nothing else will do, especially in relationships.

Time is indispensable; all work requires an expenditure of time.

Time is essential for accomplishment of all kinds. How are you using yours?

Devote uninterrupted chunks of time to the most important people in your life.

Remember, it's quantity of time at home, and quality of time at work, that counts.

Avoid making decisions on matters that don't need decisions. If it is not necessary to decide, it is necessary not to decide.

Build wisdom and confidence in others by forcing them to think and decide for themselves.

"Control your destiny or someone else will."
—Jack Welch, CEO General Electric Company

All strategic planning is ultimately customer planning.

The first quality of courage is the willingness to launch with no guarantees. The second quality of courage is the ability to endure when there is no success in sight.

Use mindstorming regularly. Define your goal in a form of a question and write out 20 answers to it.

The *Law of Forced Efficiency* says, "There is always enough time to do the most important things."

Incompetent employees undermine your credibility, sabotage your future.

Everything you do involves a choice between what is more important and what is less important. Choose well.

<∰>

"Dehiring" is a key part of leadership. The person who keeps an incompetent employee in place is himself incompetent.

"If you aren't fired with enthusiasm, you will be fired with enthusiasm."
—Vince Lombardi, football coach

Be willing to admit you've made a poor choice—33 percent of employees don't work out over time.

Leaders are firm, but fair and decisive when a person doesn't work out at the job.

The leader sets the tone for the whole organization. Morale always flows from the top.

<⬧>

Leaders are strategic thinkers. They can see the "big picture."

Leaders are innovative, entrepreneurial, and future-oriented. They focus on getting the job done.

Leaders have an obsession with customer service.

Leaders never use the word "failure." They look upon setbacks as learning experiences.

Leaders are anticipatory thinkers. They consider all consequences of their behaviors before they act.

What has been responsible for your greatest successes in life to date? Find out what it is and then do more of it.

The future belongs to the competent. Get good, get better, be the best!

Imagine if your business burned down and you had to walk across the street and start again, what would you do differently?

React quickly to changes in the situation.
When you get new information, make
new decisions.

Optimism is the one quality more
associated with success and happiness
than any other.

Work all the time you work! Don't fool around—set an example for others.

The keys to great victories are usually speed, surprise, and concentration. They work in business, too.

Speed is one of the most important qualities of leadership.

Entrepreneurial leadership requires the ability to move quickly when opportunity presents itself.

< ❀ >

You are only as free as your options. Continually develop alternate courses of action.

Whatever your problem, define it clearly *in writing* before attempting to solve it.

Identify all the possible *causes* of a problem before you decide on a solution.

The *quality* of the solution you pick will be in direct proportion to the *quantity* of solutions you consider.

When God wants to send you a gift, He wraps it up in a problem. The bigger the problem, the bigger the gift.

Life is a continuous succession of problems. Solving simple problems is what qualifies you to solve even more complex problems.

Allow time for mental digestion. When you propose a new idea, give the person time to think about it.

Think before acting, then act quickly and decisively.

Where there is no vision, the people perish. What is your vision for yourself and your organization?

The only limits on what you can accomplish are the limits you place on your own imagination.

The person who asks questions has control. Use questions to control the conversation.

All business success is built around competitive advantage. What is yours? What should it be? Could it be?

The very worst use of time is to do very well what need not be done at all.

For maximum motivation, praise in public, appraise in private.

⋖ ✦ ⋗

Make a list of all the reasons you want to be a major success in your field; reasons are the fuel in the furnace of achievement.

Follow your personal energy cycle. Do important tasks when you are most energetic and alert.

Expand your vocabulary; learn and use new and better words every day.

Train your memory to increase your ability to retain names, numbers, facts, and information.

Your life only gets better when you do. Your staff only get better when you become a better manager. Go to work on yourself.

Information is doubling in every field every 3 to 5 years. This means your knowledge must double as well.

Everyone today has piles of information to read, but the rule is: If it's more than <u>six months old</u>, it's junk!

Of all information saved or filed, <u>80</u> percent is *never* referred to again.

Before filing or storing anything, ask
yourself if you will ever *need* this
information again.

When you have too much to do, make a
list of every single task before you begin
to get your life back under control.

Continually seek ways to increase productivity, performance, and output.

People are your most valuable asset. Only people can be made to appreciate in value.

Become the kind of person that people would follow voluntarily, even if you had no title or position.

Leadership in business is ultimately expressed in financial results. Continually seek ways to increase revenues or reduce costs.

Stand in front of a full-length mirror every morning and ask yourself if you see a top professional looking back at you.

Universal
Laws of
Success

The Law of Cause and Effect

Everything happens for a reason. For every cause there is an effect, and for every effect, whether you know it or not, there is a specific cause or causes. There are no accidents.

You can have anything you want in life if you can first decide exactly what it is, and then do the things that others have done to achieve the same result.

The Law of Mind

All causation is mental. Your thoughts become your realities. Your thoughts are creative. You become what you think about most of the time.

Think continually about the things you really want, and refuse to think about the things you don't want.

The Law of Mental Equivalency

The world around you is the physical equivalent of the world within you. Your main job in life is to create within your own mind the mental equivalent of the life you want to live.

Imagine your ideal life, in every respect. Hold that thought until it materializes around you.

The Law of Correspondence

Your outer life is a reflection of your inner life. There is a direct correspondence between the way you think and feel on the inside and the way you act and experience on the outside.

Your relationships, health, wealth, and position are mirror images of your inner world.

The Law of Belief

Whatever you believe, with feeling, becomes your reality. You do not believe what you see; you see what you have already chosen to believe.

You must identify, then remove the self-limiting beliefs that hold you back.

The Law of Values

You always act in a manner consistent with your innermost values and convictions.

What you say and do, the choices you make—especially under stress—are an exact expression of what you truly value, regardless of what you say.

The Law of Motivation

Everything you do or say is triggered by your inner desires, drives, and instincts. These may be conscious or unconscious.

The key to success is to set your own goals and determine your own motivations.

The Law of Subconscious Activity

Your subconscious mind makes all your words and actions fit a pattern consistent with your self-concept and your innermost beliefs about yourself.

Your subconscious mind will move you forward or hold you back depending on how you program it.

The Law of Expectations

Whatever you expect with confidence tends to materialize in the world around you.

You always act in a manner consistent with your expectations, and your expectations influence the attitudes and behaviors of the people around you.

The Law of Concentration

Whatever you dwell upon grows and expands in your life. Whatever you concentrate upon and think about repeatedly increases in your world.

Therefore, you must focus your thinking on the things you really want in your life.

The Law of Habit

Fully 95 percent of everything you do is the result of your habits, either helpful or hurtful.

You can develop habits of success by practicing and repeating success behaviors over and over until they become automatic.

The Law of Attraction

You continually attract into your life the people, ideas, and circumstances that harmonize with your dominant thoughts, either positive or negative.

You can be, have, and do more because you can change your dominant thoughts.

The Law of Choice

Your life is the sum total of all your choices up to this present minute.

Since you are always free to choose what you think about, you are in complete control of your life and everything that happens to you.

The Law of Optimism

A positive mental attitude is essential for success and happiness in every area of life.

Your attitude is an expression of your values, beliefs, and expectations.

The Law of Change

Change is inevitable. Because it is driven by expanding knowledge and technology, it is accelerating at a speed never seen before.

Your job is to be a master of change rather than a victim of change.

The Law of Control

You feel positive about yourself to the degree to which you feel you are in control of your own life.

Health, happiness, and high performance begin with your taking complete control over your thinking, your actions and your circumstances in the world around you.

The Law of Responsibility

You are *where* you are and *what* you are
because of *you.*

You are fully responsible for everything
you are, everything you have, and
everything you become.

The Law of Compensation

The universe is completely balanced and in perfect order. You will always be compensated in full for everything you do.

You will get out what you put in. You can have more because you can contribute more.

The Law of Service

Your rewards in life will be in direct proportion to the value of your service to others.

The more you work, study, and develop your ability to contribute more to the lives and well-being of others, the better life you will have in all areas.

The Law of Applied Effort

All your hopes, dreams, goals, and aspirations are amenable to hard work.

The harder you work, the luckier you get.

There are no shortcuts.

The Law of Preparation

Luck is when opportunity meets preparation. Perfect performance comes from painstaking preparation, often for weeks, months, and years in advance.

The most successful people in every area invariably spend far more time in preparation than the least successful.

The Law of Forced Efficiency

There is never enough time to do everything, but there is always enough time to do the most important things.

The more you take on, the more efficient you become. You only learn how much you can actually do by trying to do too much.

The Law of Decision

Decisiveness is a vital quality of all successful people.

Every great leap forward in your life comes after you have made a clear decision of some kind.

The Law of Creativity

"Whatever the mind of man can conceive and believe, it can achieve."
—Napoleon Hill, success author

Every advance in your life begins with an idea of some kind, and since your ability to generate new ideas is unlimited, your future can be unlimited as well.

The Law of Flexibility

Be clear about your goals; be flexible about the process of achieving them.

Flexibility and adaptability are the core qualities for success in an age of rapid change, competition, and obsolescence.

The Law of Persistence

Your ability to persist in the face of adversities, setbacks, and disappointments is your measure of your belief in yourself.

Persistence is the iron quality of success; if you persist long enough you must eventually succeed.

The Law of Integrity

Happiness and high performance come to you when you choose to live your life consistent with your highest values and your deepest convictions.

Always be true to the very best that is within you.

The Law of Emotion

You are 100-percent emotional in everything you think, feel, and decide. You decide emotionally and justify logically.

No one *makes* you feel anything. It is how you react and respond that determines your emotions.

The Law of Happiness

The quality of your life is determined by how you feel at any given moment. How you feel is determined by how you interpret what is happening around you, not by the events themselves.

It's never too late·to have a happy childhood. At any time, you can go back and change the way you interpret those experiences to yourself.

The Law of Substitution

Your conscious mind can only hold one thought at a time, positive or negative. You can decide to be happy by substituting positive thoughts for negative ones.

Your mind is like a garden. Either weeds or flowers will grow.

The Law of Expression

Whatever is expressed is impressed. Whatever you say to yourself with emotion generates thoughts, ideas, and behaviors consistent with those words.

Be sure to talk about the things you want, and refuse to talk about the things you don't want.

The Law of Reversibility

Your thoughts and feelings determine your actions, and your actions, in turn, determine your thoughts and feelings.

By acting in a positive, pleasant, and optimistic way, you become a positive, optimistic, and enjoyable person.

The Law of Visualization

The world around you is an outpicturing of the world within you. The images you dwell upon affect your thoughts, feelings, and behavior.

Whatever you visualize clearly and emotionally will eventually materialize in your world.

The Law of Practice

Whatever you practice over and over becomes a new habit. You can develop the attitudes, abilities, and qualities of happiness and success by repeating them until they are firmly entrenched as part of your personality.

The Law of Commitment

The quality of love and the duration of a relationship are in direct proportion to the depth of the commitment by both people to making the relationship successful.

Commit yourself wholeheartedly and unconditionally to the most important people in your life.

The Law of Compatibility

You are invariably attracted to, and most compatible with, people who have the same values, beliefs, and convictions that you do—love is not blind.

Look for someone who thinks and feels the way you do about the most important issues of life.

The Law of Communications

The quality of your relationships will be determined by the quality and quantity of your communication with other people.

Good communications require extended periods of time to build and maintain.

The Law of Attention

You pay attention to that which you most love and value.

Attentive listening to others lets them know that you love them and builds trust, the foundation of a loving relationship.

The Law of Self-Esteem

Everything you do in life is to either increase or protect your self-esteem. You tend to be happiest with someone who makes you feel valuable and important.

The more things you do to raise the self-esteem of another, the more you like and respect yourself as well.

The Law of Indirect Effort

You will be more successful indirectly in relationships rather than directly. To have a friend, be a friend. To impress others, be impressed by them.

To develop and maintain loving relationships, become a loving person yourself.

The Law of Reverse Effort

The harder you try to force a relationship to work, the less successful it will be.

Relationships work best when you simply relax, be yourself, and enjoy the moment.

The Law of Identification

Hypersensitivity, or taking things personally, is a major source of problems in relationships.

Only by not identifying, by detaching and viewing your relationship with some objectivity, can you enjoy it fully and act effectively within it.

The Law of Forgiveness

You are emotionally healthy to the exact degree to which you can freely forgive others for anything they may have done that has hurt you in any way.

The inability to forgive lies at the root of most unhappiness. It leads to feelings of guilt, resentment, anger, and hostility toward others.

The Law of Reality

People don't change. Deal with them as they are. Don't try to change others or expect them to change. "What you see is what you get."

Unconditional acceptance of others is the key to happy relationships.

The Law of Minimum Effort

You always try to get the things you want with the very least effort possible. All technological advances are ways of getting greater output with less input.

All human beings are therefore basically lazy, seeking the easiest way possible at all times.

The Law of Maximization

You always try to get the very most in exchange for your time, money, effort, or emotions. When given a choice between more or less for the same contribution, you will always choose more.

People are therefore basically greedy in everything they do. This is neither good nor bad in itself. It just is.

The Law of Expediency

You always try to get the things you want as quickly and as easily as possible with minimum regard to secondary consequences.

You tend to follow the path of least resistance in everything you do.

The Law of Duality

You always give one of two reasons for doing anything—the reason that sounds good, or the real reason.

The reason that sounds good is always uplifting and noble. The real reason is because your action is the fastest and easiest way to get the things you want, right now.

The Law of Choice

Everything you do is a choice based on your dominant values at the moment. Even taking no action is a choice.

You are where you are and what you are because of your choices and decisions in life to this moment.

The Law of Subjective Value

All value is in the eye of the beholder. There is no set value for anything. Something is only worth what someone else is willing to pay.

The person willing to pay ultimately determines the true value of any item.

The Law of Time Preference

You always prefer earlier rather than later in the satisfaction of any desire.

You are therefore impatient in virtually every area of your life.

The Law of Marginality

The ultimate price of any product or service is determined by what the last customers are willing to pay for the last items available.

Every sale, or markdown of prices, is an admission that the vendor guessed wrongly when setting the original prices.

The Law of Supply and Demand

When the quantity of goods or resources is limited, an increase in the price will lead to a decrease in the demand, and vice versa.

Whatever you reward you get more of, whatever you punish you get less of. Taxes and regulations are punishment for productive activities. Welfare and benefits are rewards for unproductive activities.

Cohen`s Law

Everything is negotiable.

Every price or term, whether buying or selling, is a best-guess by someone as to what the market will bear.

Always ask for a better price.

Dawson`s Law

You can always get a better deal if you know how to ask for it in the best possible way.

Always ask for more than you want. Never accept the first price quoted. Be patient, and then ask for more.

The Law of Timing

Timing is a critical aspect of any negotiation. Whenever you make an offer, give a deadline for acceptance.

On the other hand, if someone tries to give you a deadline to accept a deal, simply say, "If that's all the time I have, then the answer is no."

The Law of Terms

The terms of payment in a negotiation can be more important than price, or any other factor.

You can usually agree to almost any price if you can get very favorable terms.

The Law of Preparation

Eighty percent of success in negotiating is determined by the preparation you do, in advance.

Before negotiating, be sure to get the facts, do your homework, and check your assumptions.

The Law of Reversal

Before negotiating, put yourself in the other person's position and negotiate from his point of view.

When you develop a good feel for the situation of the other person, you can more effectively negotiate the best deal for yourself.

The Law of Desire

The one who most wants the negotiation to succeed has the least bargaining power.

You can only negotiate effectively on your own behalf when you are willing to walk away if the price or terms are unsatisfactory.

The Law of Reciprocity

People are inherently fair and are motivated to pay you back for any nice things you do for them.

By making small concessions in a negotiation, you may be able to get large concessions in return.

The Law of Finality

No negotiation is ever final. If you get new information, or you are unhappy with the agreed upon terms, ask to reopen the negotiation.

Be willing to adjust the price and terms for the other person as well, if he or she is unhappy.

The Law of Abundance

We live in an abundant universe where there is an ample supply of money for all those who really want it.

To achieve financial independence, make a decision today to accumulate wealth and then do what others have done before you to accomplish the same goal.

The Law of Exchange

Money is the medium of exchange between the goods and services produced by one person and the goods and services produced by another.

The amount you earn at any time is a reflection of the value that others place upon your contribution.

The Law of Capital

Capital represents assets that can be deployed to generate cash flow. Your most valuable asset is your earning ability.

Your physical, mental, and intellectual resources—continually growing and changing—are your personal capital.

The Law of Saving

Pay yourself first. Financial freedom comes to those who save 10 percent or more of their income throughout their lives.

If you cannot save money, the seeds of greatness are not in you.

The Law of Conservation

It's not how much you make but how much you keep that counts.

Successful people save in prosperous times so they have a financial cushion in times of recession.

Parkinson`s Law

Expenses always rise to meet income. This is why most people retire poor.

To become wealthy, you must spend less than you earn, and save the balance.

The Law of Investing

Investigate before you invest. Spend as much time studying an investment as you do earning the money you put into it.

Never let yourself be rushed into an irrevocable financial commitment.

The Law of Compound Interest

Accumulating money and allowing it to grow at compound interest will make you rich.

The key to achieving financial independence through saving is to put the money away and never touch it, for any reason.

The Law of Accumulation

Great financial achievement is an accumulation of hundreds, and even thousands, of small efforts that no one ever sees or appreciates.

There is no quick or easy way to become rich.

The Law of Attraction

As you accumulate money, you begin attracting more money into your life.

Thinking positively about your money as you save it turns you into a money magnet. More money comes to you.

The Law of Desire

To become wealthy, you must have a burning desire to accumulate wealth. A mild desire or casual interest is not sufficient.

You can tell how badly you want it by observing your actions each day. Are they consistent with wealth accumulation?

The Law of Purpose

Definitiveness of purpose is the starting point of all wealth. To become wealthy, you must decide exactly what you want, write it down and then make a plan for its accomplishment.

All successful people "think on paper."

The Law of Enrichment

All lasting wealth comes from enriching others in some way.

The more you can train yourself to contribute value to the lives of others, the more you will earn and the more certain it is that you will become wealthy.

The Law of Entrepreneurship

The surest road to wealth is to start and build a successful business of your own. No one ever got rich working for someone else.

Your products or services only need to be 10 percent better than your competitors to start you on the road to wealth.

The Law of Bootstrapping

The best and surest way to build a business is to start with little or nothing, and then to grow step-by-step out of your profits.

Those who start with too little money are more likely to succeed than those who start with too much. Energy and imagination are the springboards to wealth creation.

The Law of Courage

Your willingness to risk failure is the only real measure of your desire to be rich.

Failure is a prerequisite for great success.

"Do you want to be successful faster? Then double your rate of failure."
—Thomas J. Watson, Sr., founder of IBM

The Law of Risk

There is a direct relationship between the level of risk and the likelihood of loss in any enterprise.

Successful entrepreneurs are those who analyze and minimize risk in the pursuit of profit.

The Law of Undue Optimism

Excessive optimism is a two-edged sword; it can lead to both success and failure.

In business, everything costs twice as much as you expect and takes three times longer than you planned.

The Law of Persistence

If you persist long enough in the pursuit of wealth, you must inevitably succeed.

Stumbling blocks are stepping stones to success, as long as you learn from every setback and disappointment.

The Law of Purpose in Business

The purpose of a business is to create and keep a customer. All business activities must be focused on this central purpose.

Profits are a result of creating and keeping customers in a cost-effective way.

The Law of Organization

A business organization is a group of people brought together for the sole purpose of creating and keeping customers.

Every employee must be essential to the functions of the organization.

The Law of Customer Satisfaction

Everyone is in the business of customer satisfaction, and the customer is always right.

Successful businesses have an obsession with customer service.

The Law of the Customer

Customers always seek the very most at the lowest possible price.

Proper business planning demands that you focus on the self-interest of the customer at all times.

The Law of Quality

Quality is whatever the customer thinks it is, and the customer decides how much it's worth.

Your ability to add value to your product or service determines your success in the market.

The Law of Obsolescence

If it works, it's obsolete.

Every product and service today is already in the process of being made obsolete by technology and competition. What is your "next miracle" going to be?

The Law of Innovation

One good idea is all you need to start a fortune.

Business breakthroughs come from finding faster, cheaper, better, easier ways to perform a task.

The Law of Critical Success Factors

Every business or position has no more than five to seven critical success factors that determine how well it does.

Identify the critical things you do that determine your success or failure. Make a plan to get better at each one of them.

The Law of the Market

The true price of anything is what someone is willing to pay for it in an open, competitive market with other alternatives available.

The market is always right.

The Law of Specialization

To succeed in business, you must specialize in a particular product or service for a particular customer, and then do what you do in an excellent fashion.

A primary reason for business failure is a loss of focus.

The Law of Differentiation

Every product or service must be different and better in some unique way to succeed in a competitive marketplace.

Your competitive advantage must be perceivable, promotable, and something the market will pay for.

The Law of Segmentation

Business success comes from identifying and targeting specific customer groups or market segments for your product or service.

Who exactly is your customer? Where is he or she? Why does he or she buy?

The Law of Market Concentration

Market success comes from concentrating single-mindedly on those specific customers who can most benefit from the unique competitive advantages of your product or service.

Identifying and focusing your efforts on this core group is the key to profitability.

The Law of Excellence

The market only pays excellent rewards for excellent performance, excellent products, or excellent service.

Identifying and developing your "area of excellence" is the first job of management.

The Law of Probability

Every event has some probability of occurring. To increase the chances of an event occurring, increase the number of events.

The more times and the more different things you try, the more likely it is that you will succeed.

The Law of Clarity

The clearer you are about what you want, and what you are willing to do to get it, the more likely it is that you will be lucky and get what you want.

Clarity of desired goals is a magnet that draws good luck to you.

The Law of Expectations

You increase the amount of luck in your life by continuously expecting lucky things to happen to you.

Begin every day by saying, "I believe that something wonderful is going to happen to me today!"

The Law of Opportunity

Your greatest possibilities will often come from the most common situations around you.

Your biggest opportunity probably lies under your own feet, in your current job, industry, education, experience, or interests.

The Law of Ability

Luck is what happens when preparedness meets opportunity.

The more ability you have and develop in any field, the more likely it is that lucky breaks will occur for you.

The Law of Integrative Complexity

The person with the widest variety of knowledge and skill in any area will have the most luck in that area.

Expanded knowledge and skill intensify awareness and expand opportunity.

The Law of Assumption

Incorrect assumptions lie at the root of every failure. Have the courage to test your assumptions.

The willingness to accept the possibility that you could be wrong will open you to possibilities and lucky breaks you might otherwise miss.

The Law of Timing

Timing is everything. With proper preparation, the right time will come for you.

"There is a tide in the affairs of men which, taken at the flood, leads on to fortune."
—William Shakespeare

The Law of Energy

The greater the energy and enthusiasm you have, the more likely it is that you will recognize and respond to luck.

Your best ideas and most profound insights come after a period of rest and relaxation.

The Law of Relationships

The more people you know and who know you in a positive way, the luckier you will be.

People will give you ideas and open doors for you if they like you.

The Law of Empathy

When you look at a situation through the eyes of someone else, you often find unseen possibilities.

What is it that people need and want, and how could you give it to them?

The Law of Growth

If you are not growing, you are stagnating. If you are not getting better, you are getting worse.

Make continuous learning and growth a part of your daily routine.

The Law of Practice

Practice is the price of mastery. Whatever you practice over and over again becomes a new habit of thought and performance.

Growth and fulfillment come from abandoning old practices and embracing new ones.

The Law of Accumulation

A great life is an accumulation of thousands of efforts and sacrifices unseen by others.

"Those heights by great men won and kept, were not achieved by sudden flight. But they, while their companions slept were toiling upward in the night."
—Henry Wadsworth Longfellow

The Law of Self-Development

You can learn anything you need to learn to achieve virtually any goal that you can set for yourself.

Those who learn, can.

The Law of Talents

You contain within yourself a unique combination of talents and abilities which, properly identified and applied, will enable you to achieve virtually any goal you can set for yourself.

What parts of your work do you enjoy the most, and are you the best at? This is your best indicator of your true talents.

The Law of Excellence

Success and happiness are only possible when you become absolutely excellent at doing something you enjoy.

"The quality of your life will be determined by your commitment to excellence more than by any other factor."
—Vince Lombardi

The Law of Opportunity

Difficulties come not to obstruct, but to instruct. Within every setback or obstacle lie seeds of an equal or greater benefit or opportunity.

What appears to be your biggest problem in life may disguise your greatest opportunity.

The Law of Courage

The systematic, deliberate development of courage is essential to the achievement of success. Fear is the greatest single obstacle to achievement.

Make a habit of always confronting the things you fear and doing them anyway.

The Law of Applied Effort

All great success and achievement is preceded and accompanied by hard, hard work. When in doubt, try harder. And if that doesn't work, try harder still.

And when you work, work all the time you work! Don't waste time.

The Law of Giving

The more you give of yourself without expectation of return, the more good that will come back to you, from the most unexpected sources.

You will only be truly happy when you feel that you are making a real difference in the world by serving others in some way.

The Law of Affirmation

Fully 95 percent of your thinking and feeling is determined by the way you talk to yourself. Your inner dialogue is accepted as commands by your subconscious mind.

Talk to yourself positively and constructively all the time, even when you don't feel like it.

The Law of Optimism

How you think, feel, and behave is determined by how you interpret your experiences to yourself.

When you make a habit of looking for the good in every situation, you develop a positive mental attitude and eventually you become unstoppable.

About the Author

Brian Tracy is a world authority on the development of human potential and personal effectiveness. He teaches his key ideas, methods, and techniques on peak performance to more than 100,000 people every year, showing them how to double and triple their productivity and get their lives into balance at the same time. This book contains some to the best leadership concepts ever discovered.

These other Successories® titles are available from Career Press:

- *Great Little Book for The Peak Performance Woman*
- *Great Little Book on Mastering Your Time*
- *Great Little Book on Successful Selling*
- *The Power of Goals*
- *Winning with Teamwork*
- *Commitment to Excellence*
- *The Best of Success*
- *The Essence of Attitude*
- *The Magic of Motivation*
- *Great Quotes from Great Women*
- *Great Quotes from Great Sports Heroes*
- *Great Quotes from Great Leaders*
- *Great Quotes from Zig Ziglar*

To order call: 1-800-CAREER-1 (1-800-227-3371)

Other best-selling audio/video programs
by Brian Tracy

- *Action Strategies for Personal Achievement*
  (24 audios / workbook)
- Universal Laws of Success & Achievement
  (8 audios / workbook)
- *Psychology of Achievement*
  (audios / workbook)

To order call: 1-800-542-4252

Brian Tracy takes achievement to new heights in...
Maximum Achievement
(352 pages), Simon & Schuster

Brian Tracy's best-selling book takes 2,500 years of ideas on success and achievement and condenses them into a simple system you can use to transform your life. More than a million men and women, in 16 languages, in 31 countries, are already using Brian's powerful ideas, methods and techniques to increase their incomes, improve their relationships and unlock their potentials for happier, healthier living. This exciting book will show you how to set and achieve you goals faster than you ever thought possible. Order it today! ($12 paperback.)

To order call: 800-793-9552.